SALMON on TOAST

BY: **D.J.VANDOR**

ILLUSTRATED BY: **BONNIE LEMAIRE**

Salmon on Toast
Copyright © 2020 by D. J. Vandor

Tellwell Talent
www.tellwell.ca

ISBN
978-0-2288-3213-3 (Hardcover)
978-0-2288-3212-6 (Paperback)
978-0-2288-3214-0 (eBook)

FOR SOPHIE AND SAMMY

WHEN LIFE CLOSES A DOOR, OPEN THE PANTRY.

HE HAS BIG ROUND EYES
THAT BOUNCE UP AND DOWN
AND A TUFT OF RED HAIR,
WHICH HE COMBS WITH CARE.

HE LOOKS KIND OF SHINY
BECAUSE HE'S SO SLIMY.
HE IS CUTE FOR A SLUG.
HIS FRIENDS CALL HIM PUG.

HE LIVES IN A HOUSE
AT THE TOP OF A HILL.
IT OVERLOOKS A LARGE BAY,
AND IT'S MADE OF RED CLAY.

NOW MOST OTHER SLUGS
LIVE IN HOLES THEY HAVE DUG.
BUT NOT PUG.
HE'S A DIFFERENT KIND OF SLUG.

PUG LOVES TO EAT.
HE ESPECIALLY LIKES FISH.
AND THE ONE HE LOVES MOST
IS SALMON ON TOAST.

BUT PUG HAS A PROBLEM.
HE'S MISPLACED HIS CAN OPENER,
AND HE'S IN QUITE A MOOD.
PUG IS STARTING TO BROOD.

HE TRIES HITTING THE CAN,
SMASHING IT HARD WITH A PAN,
DROPPING IT ONTO THE FLOOR,
THROWING IT STRAIGHT AT THE DOOR!

PUG NEEDS A PLAN
IF HE WANTS TO EAT
THE DISH HE LOVES MOST,
SALMON ON TOAST.

FISHING IN THE BAY
SEEMS THE EASIEST WAY
TO GET SOME FISH
FOR HIS FAVOURITE DISH.

ALL AT ONCE,
PUG STARTS TO GRIN.
HE'S THOUGHT IT THROUGH.
HE KNOWS WHAT TO DO.

PUG FINDS A STRONG STICK,
WHICH HE JOINS TO SOME TWINE.
THIS FINE PIECE OF TWINE
WILL ACT AS A LINE.

TO WHICH HE ATTACHES
A HOOK THAT WILL CATCH
THE DISH HE LOVES MOST—
SALMON ON TOAST.

PUG NEEDS SOME BAIT
TO CATCH SOMETHING GREAT.
HE DIGS FOR A WORM.
LOOK AT IT SQUIRM!

HURRYING DOWN TO THE BAY
WITHOUT FURTHER DELAY,
HE IS RATHER DELIGHTED.
HE'S QUITE EXCITED.

WITH ALL OF HIS STRENGTH,
HE THRUSTS OUT THE LINE,
BUT IT CATCHES IN SOME REEDS.
OH! PUG IS PEEVED!

HE TUGS AND HE LUGS
AND FINALLY, HE SHRUGS.
HE PULLS AT HIS HAIR
AND BEGINS TO DESPAIR.

WHILE FRETTING ABOUT,
HE NOTICES THE SNOUTS,
THEN THE BEAUTIFUL TAILS
OF TWO LARGE SPOTTED WHALES.

THE INCREDIBLE PAIR
SAIL INTO THE AIR,
REACHING SUCH A GREAT HEIGHT,
THEY APPEAR TO TAKE FLIGHT.

BUT DOWN THEY DO CRASH,
SPLASH!
CREATING A WAVE,
WHICH STARTS TO GROW,
INCREASINGLY SO!

GATHERING SPEED,
IT RUMBLES,
IT ROARS!
IT CRASHES ONTO THE SHORE!

IT WASHES OVER PUG,
LIFTING HIM UP AND AWAY.
HE TRIES TO SHOUT.
HE COUGHS. HE SPUTTERS. HE FLOATS ABOUT.

HIS LIFE VEST ON TIGHT,
HE IS QUITE A SIGHT
AS HE PRAYS AND HE HOPES
FOR A SWIFT RESCUE BOAT.

BUT AS QUICK AS IT CAME,
THE WAVE LEAVES IN A FLASH.
LEAVING PUG ALONE IN THE MUD
FEELING RATHER QUITE GLUM.

HE'S BACK WHERE HE STARTED,
UNABLE TO MAKE
THE DISH HE LOVES MOST-
SALMON ON TOAST.

SO HOME PUG DOES CRAWL,
EMPTY-HANDED AND WET,
FEELING NOT VERY CLEVER
AND HUNGRIER THAN EVER.

HE CRAWLS INTO HIS HOUSE.
WHAT A WET GLOOMY DAY!
NOT ONE SINGLE FISH.
NO FAVOURITE DISH.

PUG FROWNS. HE IS CROSS.
FOR SO MUCH HE HAS LOST.
AND HE STILL HAS TO EAT,
DESPITE HIS FAILED FISHING FEAT!

OPENING WIDE, THE PANTRY DOOR,
PUG REACHES FOR SOME FOOD,
AND GUESS WHAT FALLS TO THE FLOOR?
THE CAN OPENER!

YAY!
HOORAY!
HURRY UP!
LET'S EAT!

HE OPENS FIVE CANS,
STACKING THEM TALL ON HIS TOAST,
AND BEFORE THEY FALL OVER,
(IT'S ALL VERY TIPPY)
HE GOBBLES THEM UP.
IT HAPPENS QUITE QUICKLY.

WITH A SMILE ON HIS FACE
AND A FULL, HAPPY TUMMY,
PUG THINKS SALMON ON TOAST
HAS NEVER TASTED THIS ...

YUMMY.

ABOUT THE AUTHOR

D.J.Vandor is a retired Olympic rower who likes to write silly stories. He lives in Vancouver with his ~~silly~~ wife and his two silly children.
smart and beautiful

ABOUT THE ILLUSTRATOR

Illustrator Bonnie Lemaire delights readers by making comical and curious characters dance on the page. Her illustrations have brought smiles to many young (and old) faces all over the world.

CPSIA information can be obtained
at www.ICGtesting.com
Printed in the USA
LVHW071158191120
672055LV00040B/1646

9 780228 832126